# ESPERANZA

Written and Illustrated by
Tia Ida Lulu

Dedicated to my nieces and nephews who inspire me to live courageously, and to my dear husband who supports all my wild adventures.

Esperanza the butterfly lives in the Tree of Many Colors. Orange butterflies, yellow butterflies and even blue butterflies live there.

Today, she will explore around the tree but finds that she is a little scared to go on her adventure.

Mama: Good Morning, Esperanza! Today you will explore around the tree all by yourself. Are you excited?
Esperanza: Good Morning, Mama! Yes, I am excited but I am a little scared too.

Mama: My sweet Esperanza, I understand how you feel. Sometimes, I get scared, too, when I am about to do something new.
Esperanza: How do you make the scariness go away, Mama?

Mama: I do something that makes me happy. Flying makes me happy so when I get scared, I fly and it helps the scariness go away. What makes you happy, Esperanza?

Esperanza thinks for a second…

Esperanza: hmmm…FLOWERS! Flowers make me happy!

Mama: Perfect! If you get scared on your adventure, sit on a flower.

Esperanza: Sounds like a plan! I am ready for my adventure. Thanks, Mama!

Flap…

…flap…

…flap…

Esperanza starts her adventure.

As she flies further away, she begins to get a little scared.  She remembers what her mama said and looks for a flower.

She finds a daisy to sit on and slowly the scariness starts to go away.

It worked!

Suddenly, she hears a voice calling from below.

Kazuko: Hello, butterfly! I noticed you sitting on the daisy. Are you okay?

Esperanza: Hi, Turtle. Yes, I am doing great! Today is my first day exploring and I got a little scared. Flowers make me happy, so I sat on this daisy for a while to make the scariness go away. Thank you for asking if I was okay.

What is your name?

Kazuko:  My name is Kazuko.  I live in the pond behind the Tree of Many Colors.  I never thought about being around flowers to make the scariness go away. What a great idea.  When I am scared, I imagine breathing in sunshine. What is your name, butterfly?

Esperanza: My name is Esperanza. Breathing in sunshine sounds like fun!

Kazuko: Would you like to play near the pond with me?

Esperanza: I would love to!

Esperanza and Kazuko play in the pond and enjoy the sunshine. Kazuko swims around in the water and Esperanza flies happily above her. They have fun sharing stories and giggling.

Suddenly, they see a nearby bush rustling and get scared.

Esperanza: Let's make the scariness go away by sitting on flowers and breathing sunshine!

Kazuko: Great idea!

Esperanza lands on a lily pad and touches the waterlily.  Kazuko breathes in some sunshine.

S...L...O...W...L...Y...breathing in through their nose, and then S...L...O...W...L...Y...breathing out through their mouths.

With their new courage, Esperanza and Kazuko start moving toward the rustling bush.  They peek inside and what a delightful surprise...

...they see a beautiful rainbow tailed squirrel.

Esperanza: Hi, squirrel! What are you doing hiding in the bush?

Squirrel: Hi! I am playing hide-and-seek with Willie and Waylon. They are my doggie friends.

Esperanza:  Fun!  Want to hide in the Tree of Many Colors?

Squirrel:  Great idea!  What are your names?

Esperanza:  My name is Esperanza.

Kazuko:  My name is Kazuko.

Squirrel:  My name is Sage.

Esperanza, Kazuko, and Sage slowly climb up the Tree of Many Colors. They peek around the tree and see Willie and Waylon.

Giggling, they continue climbing up the tree.

A little while later, they hear the wind start to whistle. Then the sun hides behind a cloud.

CA-CRACK-BOOM!

They hear a loud thunder and get scared. A storm is coming!

Esperanza: Oh no! There is not a flower for me to sit on to make the scariness go away.


Kazuko: Oh no! There is no sunshine for me to breathe in to make the scariness go away.


Sage: Don't worry, Esperanza and Kazuko. When I get scared, I think of many beautiful colors around me.

Sage curls his tail around his face to show them what it would look like.

Esperanza, Kazuko, and Sage imagine beautiful colors around them.

Sage is so sweet; he puts his tail above his new friends to protect them from the rain.

Esperanza and Kazuko were no longer scared.

After several minutes, the rain goes away. The wind calms down and the sun comes back out to shine.

Esperanza: Sage, thank you for protecting us from the rain with your tail. That was a great idea to think of beautiful colors to make the scariness go away.

It worked!


Soon, it is time for them to go home for the day.


Sage carries Kazuko and they climb back down the Tree of Many Colors. Kazuko goes back to the pond and Sage goes to the Pecan tree where his family lives.

Mama, I had so much fun today! There were times I got scared, but I did what you showed me and the scariness went away.

I met Kazuko. She is a turtle who lives in the pond nearby. She breathes sunshine to make the scariness go away.

Then we met Sage, a rainbow-tailed squirrel. He showed us how to imagine beautiful colors around you to make the scariness go away.

That was really cool, because we didn't have flowers or sunshine to use when the storm came.

Mama: Wow! Sounds like you learned several different ways to make the scariness go away AND you made a couple of friends.  What a GREAT day!

Esperanza: I agree! I am excited to explore more tomorrow.

Mama: My brave Esperanza, I look forward to hearing more of your adventures. Get some rest, Darling. Tomorrow is a new day.

Esperanza: Goodnight, Mama. I love you.

Mama: Goodnight, Esperanza. I love you, too

The End

# About Esperanza

Esperanza, which means "hope" in Spanish, is a Mexican Monarch butterfly who lives in the Tree of Many Colors. She has a strong curiosity for life and was born to bring hope with overcoming life's sometimes not-so-easy situations.

morse code for "hope"
H    O    P    E
····/———/·——·/ ·

morse code for "love"
L    O    V    E
·—··/———/···— / ·

Join Esperanza and her friends as they navigate the waves of life.

Made in the USA
San Bernardino, CA
24 October 2018